PINKFONG: BABY SHARK LITTLE RED RIDING HOOD
A CENTUM BOOK 978-1-912841-94-3
Published in Great Britain by Centum Books Ltd.
This edition published 2019.
1 3 5 7 9 10 8 6 4 2

Copyright © 2019 Smart Study Co., Ltd. All Rights Reserved.

Original Korean edition first published by Smart Study Co., Ltd.

This edition published by Centum Books Ltd in 2019 by arrangement with Smart Study Co., Ltd.

Centum Books Ltd, 20 Devon Square, Newton Abbot, Devon, TQ12 2HR, UK.

books@centumbooksltd.co.uk

CENTUM BOOKS Limited Reg. No. 07641486.

A CIP catalogue record for this book is available from the British Library.

Printed in China.

BABY SHARK
STORYBOOK SERIES

Baby Shark
Little Red Riding
Hood

centum

Baby Shark Family & Friends

Baby Shark

Baby Shark is curious about everything under the ocean. He likes singing as it helps him to be brave.

Mummy Shark

Mummy Shark has no limits to what she can do. She always listens to Baby Shark and shares a special bond with him.

Daddy Shark

Daddy Shark is a strong and mighty hunter. More than just a father, he also plays with Baby Shark like a friend.

Fish Bus

Fast and cute, Fish Bus is a reliable friend who helps Baby Shark to travel through the ocean.

Grandma Shark

Grandma Shark likes reading. A kind and thoughtful grandma, she always has time to spend with Baby Shark.

Grandpa Shark

Grandpa Shark is wise and smart. He is famous for his hot clam buns and enjoys sharing his cooking skills with Baby Shark.

In his red riding hood, Baby Shark
is off to visit Grandma Shark today.
Swishing goodbye with his tail,
Baby Shark is on his way!

Baby Shark sets out on his first journey alone.
'Travelling on Fish Bus is so much fun!'

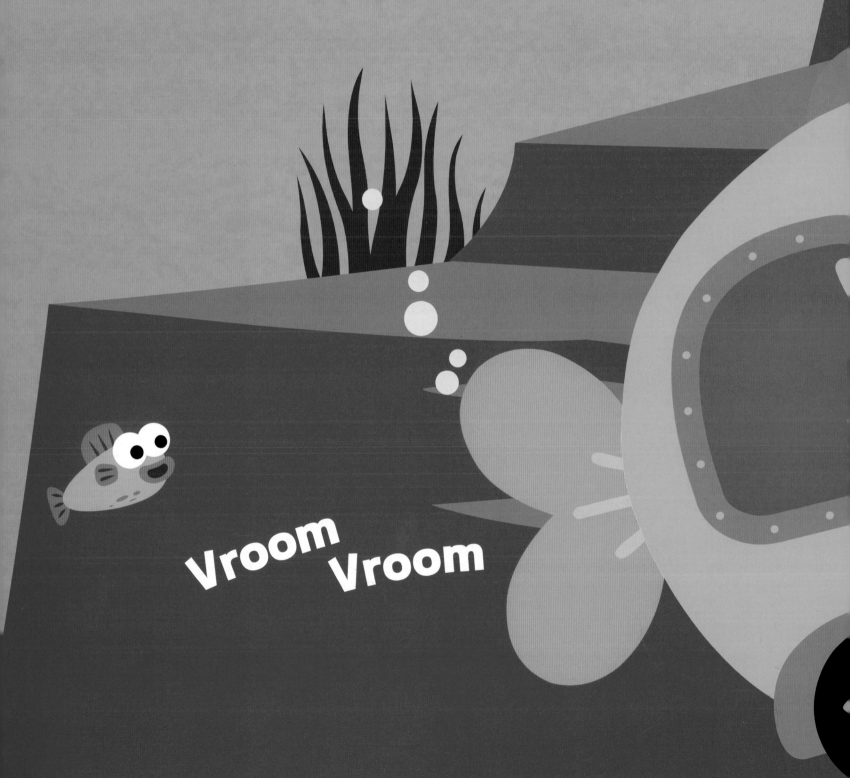

Vroom Vroom

Some playful crabs pinch Fish Bus.
'Ouch!' cries Fish Bus, as he comes
to a sudden stop.
'Let's have some fun, Baby Shark!'
say the crabs.
'No, no, crabs! I'm in a hurry,' says Baby Shark.

As the bus continues on again,
a huge whale stops them.
'I'm so bored today. Let's play, Baby Shark!'
says the whale.
'No, no! I must hurry on my way.'

'Hold on tight!' warns Fish Bus right before he speeds up.

'Oh, this is scary!' cries Baby Shark.

Take me too!

Come and play with us!

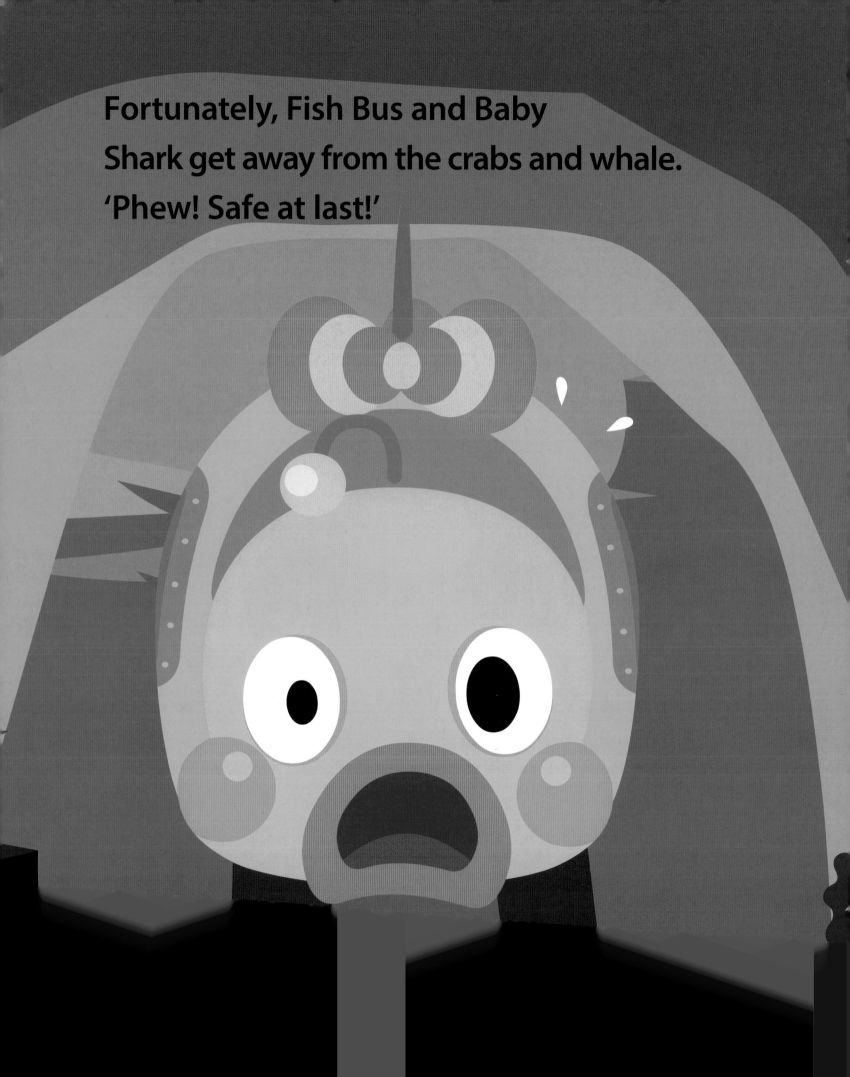

Fortunately, Fish Bus and Baby
Shark get away from the crabs and whale.
'Phew! Safe at last!'

Baby Shark doesn't realise it right away,
but now they are in a dark cave!

'It won't be so scary
if I sing my favourite song.'

Baby Shark,
doo-doo-doo-doo-doo!
Brave in the dark,
doo-doo-doo-doo-doo!

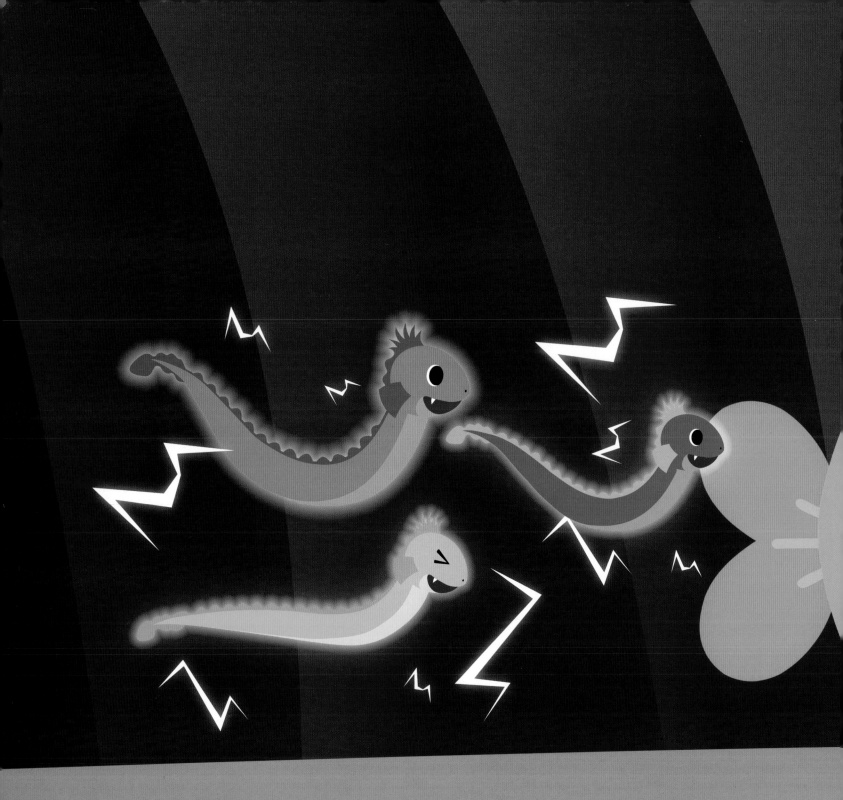

Baby Shark sees a spark in the cave so dark.

'Hi, we are electric eels! We'll light up,

so just spin your wheels!'

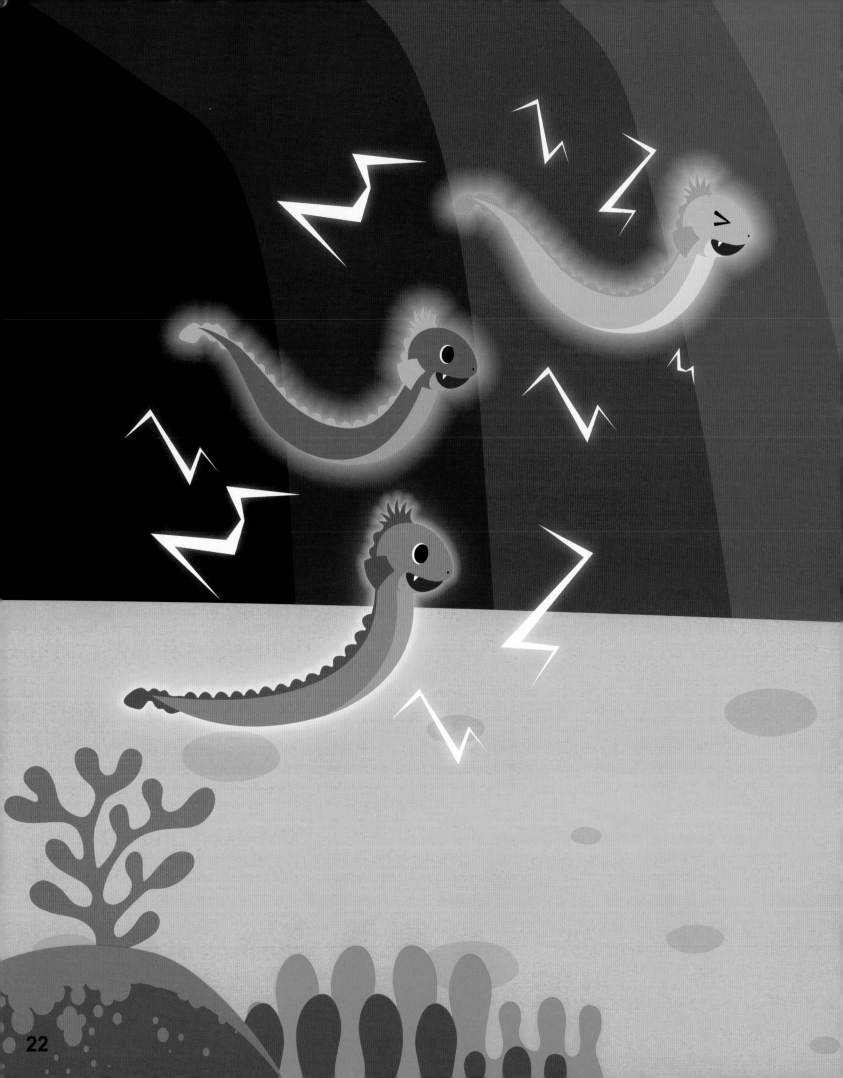

Thanks to the light, Fish Bus and Baby Shark make their way out of the dark cave.
'Thank you, eels! You are very bright.'
Once again, they are back on the right track.

They continue on under the sea.
Baby Shark misses his grandma,
and he can't wait to see her.

Finally, Baby Shark arrives.

'Grandma Shark, I've missed you so much!'

'Come give your grandma a big bear hug!'

'Thank you so much for getting him here safely,' says Grandma Shark.

'Thanks for being a good friend, Fish Bus!' says Baby Shark.

Vroom Vroom

 Baby Shark is happy to be with Grandma Shark.

Grandma Shark is happy to be with Baby Shark too.